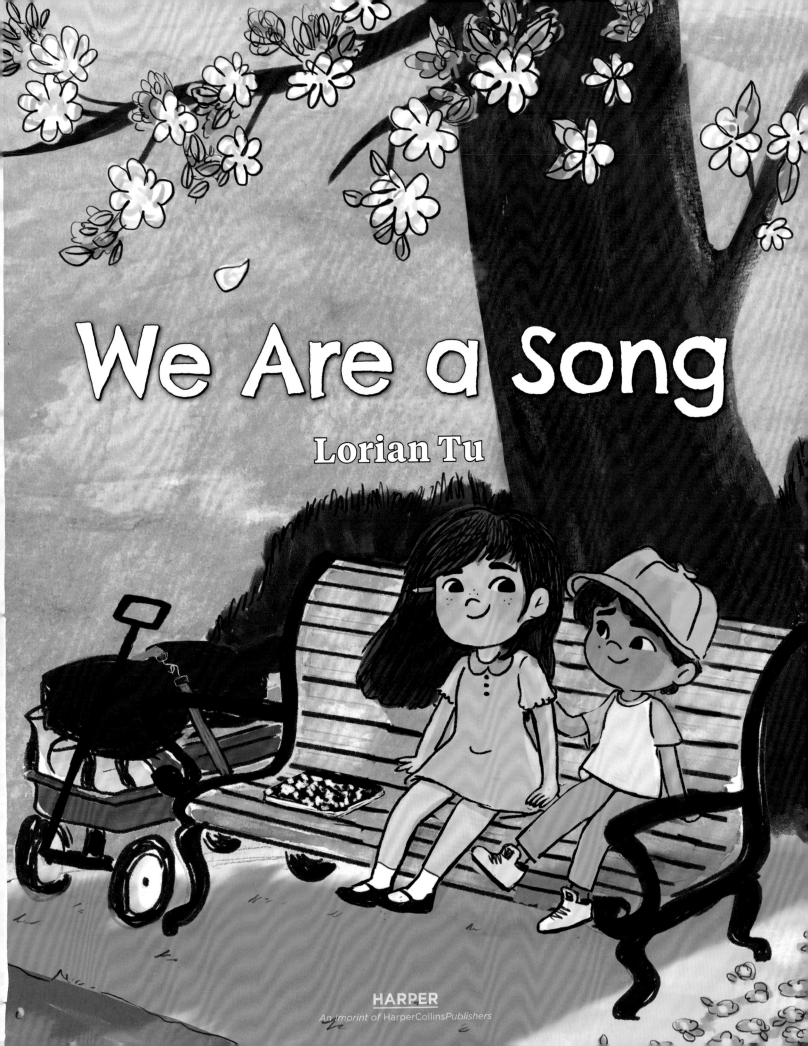

We Are a Song

Lorian Tu

HARPER
An Imprint of HarperCollins Publishers

For my family

For information address HarperCollins Children's Books,
a division of HarperCollins Publishers,
195 Broadway, New York, NY 10007.
www.harpercollinschildrens.com

Family photo in author's note courtesy of Lorian Tu.

Library of Congress Control Number: 2021953558
ISBN 978-0-06-297054-1

The artist used watercolor, gouache, ink, and colored
pencils to create the digital illustrations for this book.
Book design by Alison Klapthor
23 24 25 26 27 RTLO 10 9 8 7 6 5 4 3 2 1

First Edition

The smells from Amah's kitchen

send a cozy feeling through my whole body.

Bright green bok choy sits on the counter, freshly washed. Oil in the wok goes *ping-ping-ping*, and

Amah's ginger-slicing is like a heartbeat:

Chop-chop.

Chop-chop.

"We have a lot of work to do. The party is tonight, and the whole family will be there!" says Amah as my sister and I gulp down breakfast.

Emilyn is humming and writing in her notebook, as usual.

"I'm writing a poem for tonight, about what it means to be a family," says Emilyn.

"How nice!" Amah says. "But first, I need you to pick up some things for the party."

"I'll help!" I chime. Brothers always help.

We promise Amah we'll be back in time to

help set up for the party.

"Where are we going first?" I ask.

"To Tía Cari's bakery!" Emilyn says.

I start to drool.

"¡Hola, Tía!" We sing as we open the door.

"We are here for some cake!" I say.

"Cake . . . hmmmm. Our family is like different ingredients

all mixed together . . . ," Emilyn says.

"**Mmmmm** . . . like sugar and butter and guava!" I say.

Tía says, "I think guava should be in everything," and dances back behind the counter.

The next stop is Yeh Yeh's toy store for decorations and his famous dan tat.

Jing-a-ling! the bell rings as we enter.

"Ah! My favorite grandkids!" Yeh Yeh chuckles.

"Look at all the colors!" I say.

"Our family is like a rainbow!" Emilyn says.

"See how all these separate colors come together to make something so beautiful?"

Yeh Yeh smiles and hands us the bags of decorations and a tray of dan tat as we leave.

GO FLY A KITE SALE $10 $10

Abuelo's house is the last stop. When he sees us, he puts down his guitar and takes out a box of dominoes.

"Dominoes are like our family too, right? They're all a little different but they're all part of the same set," Emilyn says.

"Let's play!" I say.

We each win a round, then Abuelo takes a big container of pernil Cubano, my favorite, to our wagon. He stacks that and his guitar on top.

"Tell your mama I'll be there soon!" He sings.

The wagon is getting harder to pull, so we stop

for a rest on the best bench in town. The one

under the old apple tree.

"Is the poem ready yet?" I ask.

"Not yet. Something's missing," Emilyn says.

The wind whooshes and the trees sway along.

"Let's go home," I say.

I stand and let the petals fall all around me. They are so beautiful. Each one is a little bit like the others but also a little bit different.

One of them kisses my cheek before it falls to the ground. It reminds me of Mama's kisses.

Mama and Abuela are on the back deck
with our baby brother, Benji.

I don't remember being a baby, but I
remember a song Abuela would sing to me.
It's always stuck in my head. I think it lives
in my heart.

I sing as we walk toward them.

Abuela joins in. "¡Palmita de pan blanco!"

Mama giggles as we do a little dance.

My sister stops in her tracks and smiles big.

"Music!" I say.

"That's it!" Emilyn agrees. "Our family is like a song!"

And she starts to sing along as she opens her notebook.

I think about how music has different sounds that go up and down, fast and slow, long and short . . . about how it

flies through your ears and into your heart, and about how it's always been such a big part of my family. Of me.

I sit next to Emilyn as she finishes writing.

"What do you think, Arturo?" she says.

"I'm still learning how to read," I say.

"I'll help you. Sisters always help."

As we read together, I can hear my heart beat like a drum, matching the poem. I can smell Tía's pastries and see all the colors in Yeh Yeh's shop and feel the dots on Abuelo's dominoes.

"It's perfect. Everyone is going to love it," I tell my sister.

The party is full of delicious food, loud music,
and all our favorite people in one place.

Yeh Yeh and Amah hum along to Abuelo's music,
Tío's belly rumbles for more pernil Cubano, and my
cousins' laughter makes me smile bigger than ever.

At the end of the night, we sit in Papa's big chair
and read the poem to Benji.

By Emilyn

Our family is a song.

I hope you sing along.

Each person just a separate note,

together, we are strong.

Like rainbows, games, and flowers

all have their separate parts,

we are the ingredients

in each other's hearts.

We make such pretty music,

a tune forever true.

And all of it together

makes the one and only

you.

Author's Note

This story is a story about me. Not the poem writing part but the figuring out part (and definitely the writing part).

My whole life, I've tried to figure out who I am. My family is full of different backgrounds, which is fun, and I love every single person in my family. But sometimes I wasn't sure who I really was or where I fit in. Growing up, I didn't know any other kids (except my brother) who had a mixed family like mine. I felt like my family was too much and not enough all at the same time. It was frustrating and lonely. Sometimes I even wanted to pretend I didn't have a family.

But as I grew, I started to see how all the things that are part of my family are part of me too. Those things are like my own recipe that makes me special and unique. Just like a rainbow or a cake or a song, I'm made up of different parts that are wonderful when put together.

Now I'm so happy to be mixed and to have many parts of myself that make me proud. Just like the kids in this story, I want to celebrate all the things that make me me. Every family is different. Whatever your family is like, it's special.